**Jessica's no *drum*-my!**

I tapped softly and marched. Right, left. Right, left. *Tap, tap, tap, tap-tap, tap-tap-tap, taptaptaptap—*

What was happening? I was tapping faster and faster, and my feet were itching to do a jig. But behind me, the other kids started marching faster and faster too.

Winston ran into Charlie. The cymbals crashed and clattered onto the floor. Charlie ran into Jerry, Jerry bumped Lois, Lois squealed, and Elizabeth and Ellen collided. It was a mess—and it was all my fault!

# Bantam Books in the SWEET VALLEY KIDS series

# LITTLE DRUMMER GIRLS

Written by
Molly Mia Stewart

Created by
FRANCINE PASCAL

Illustrated by
Marcy Ramsey

BANTAM BOOKS
NEW YORK · TORONTO · LONDON · SYDNEY · AUCKLAND

RL 2, 005-008

LITTLE DRUMMER GIRLS
*A Bantam Book / March 1998*

*Sweet Valley High® and Sweet Valley Kids® are
registered trademarks of Francine Pascal.*

*Conceived by Francine Pascal.*

*Produced by Daniel Weiss Associates, Inc.
33 West 17th Street
New York, NY 10011.*

*Cover art by Wayne Alfano.*

ISBN: 0-553-48614-4

*Published simultaneously in the United States and Canada*

*Bantam Books are published by Bantam Books, a division of Bantam
Doubleday Dell Publishing Group, Inc. Its trademark, consisting of the
words "Bantam Books" and the portrayal of a rooster, is Registered in the
U.S. Patent and Trademark Office and in other countries. Marca
Registrada. Bantam Books, 1540 Broadway, New York, New York 10036.*

PRINTED IN THE UNITED STATES OF AMERICA

OPM      0 9 8 7 6 5 4 3 2 1

*To Louis Duszynski*

# CHAPTER 1

# Musical Maniacs

"What's that, Elizabeth?" I pointed to the big, mysterious box on the floor of room 203. "Do you think there's an animal in there?"

"I don't know, Jessica," my twin sister, Elizabeth, replied. "But I can't wait to find out!"

In case you don't know me, I'm Jessica Wakefield. Elizabeth and I are in the second grade at Sweet Valley Elementary. We both have long blond hair with bangs and blue-green eyes. We look so much alike that sometimes kids have to look at our name bracelets to tell us apart.

Our teacher, Mr. Crane, is really cool. He's always bringing neat animals to class. This morning he brought in a gigantic box and set it on the floor. Then he got called into the office. After he left, everyone in our class gathered around to stare at the box.

Charlie Cashman gave it a shake. Strange sounds floated out. A clinking sound here. A rattling sound there. A loud banging sound. A soft hissing sound.

I shivered. It sounded like a snake!

Jerry McAllister jiggled the box next. *Boom! Clang! Ding-a-ling!*

"I thought I heard something banging," Eva Simpson said.

"Maybe it's a monster." Winston Egbert growled and made a goofy monster face.

"Or a gorilla," Charlie added.

"Maybe it has something to do with St. Patrick's Day," Ellen Riteman suggested. St. Patrick's Day was coming up soon.

"Yeah. It could be a leprechaun," Lila Fowler added. Lila and Ellen are my best friends, besides Elizabeth of course. Amy Sutton and Todd Wilkins are Elizabeth's best friends.

"Hi, class!" Mr. Crane greeted us as he came in. He was wearing a white dress shirt and a tie with musical notes printed all over it.

"Mr. Crane, is there a leprechaun in the box?" Winston asked.

Mr. Crane laughed. "No. But it *does* have something to do with St. Patrick's Day." He opened the box and we all peeked inside.

"Musical instruments!" Elizabeth exclaimed.

"Cymbals!" Winston yelled.

"And flutophones!" Eva cheered.

"Look at the maracas!" Lila said. She grabbed a colorful pair of maracas from the box and shook them. They made a soft *ssss* sound.

"So *that's* what was making that snake sound," I whispered.

Mr. Crane went out into the hall and brought back a big drum. It was about half as big as me.

My twin pointed at the drum. "Look, Jess. It has 'Sweet Valley Elementary' written on the side!"

"I've seen drums like those on TV," I said. "Marching bands play them in parades."

"Are we going to learn how to play these instruments?" Ellen asked.

4

"Yes," Mr. Crane said. "We're going to practice all week."

"I want the cymbals," Jerry said.

"No, I do," Winston said.

"I want the tambourine," Sandy Ferris said.

"*I* want it," Julie Porter argued.

"Wait a minute." Mr. Crane laughed softly and held up his hands. "We'll get a chance to play *all* the instruments. Now take your seats, please. I'll show you how."

Everyone scurried to their desks. I kept my eye on the big drum. It looked like it would be fun to play.

Mr. Crane held up something that looked like a metal bar that had been bent into the shape of a triangle. "This is called a triangle."

Lila rolled her eyes. "No kidding."

"You play it by tapping it with this little stick." Mr. Crane tapped it, and a soft *ding* echoed through the room.

"That's pretty," Julie said. "I want to play *that*."

Mr. Crane held up some blocks of wood. "These are sand blocks. You can play them a couple of different ways. Slide them against each other gently for a soft sound. For a harder sound, brush them harder."

"They sound like shoes scraping on gravel," Jerry said.

"Or sandpaper," Kisho Murasaki said.

"Exactly." Mr. Crane smiled and picked up another set of wood blocks. "These wood blocks don't make scraping noises. You just hit them together like this." *Pop! Clonk! Bonk!*

"That's what it sounds like when me

6

and Jerry bump heads," Charlie said.

I groaned. Why do boys always act so *dumb?* I don't know *how* Elizabeth can stand them. She plays soccer and tag with boys during recess. I like recess too—I'm the best rope-jumper in the class. But I don't like to get dirty or play with yucky *boys!*

"These are cymbals," Mr. Crane said, holding up two big golden discs. He brought them together with a crash. "And these are finger cymbals." He held up miniature versions of the big cymbals.

"The finger cymbals are cute," Lila whispered. "They're so tiny. They'd fit right on my fingertips."

"I want to play those sticks," Ken Matthews said as Mr. Crane rubbed two ridgy wood sticks together to make a ratchety noise. Then he picked up two smooth wood sticks and banged them together. *Clack! Clack!*

My big brother, Steven, likes to bang sticks together. Only when *he* does it, it doesn't sound like music. It just gives me a headache!

Mr. Crane brought out a tape player and turned it on. "The Muffin Man" began to play. "OK, class. First we'll count the beat of the song together. Then we'll try out the instruments."

"Can't we try the instruments *now?*" Winston whined. He had his eye on the big cymbals.

"First things first," Mr. Crane replied. "OK, let's count! One, two. One, two. One, two."

We all chanted to the beat of the music. It was easy!

"Good!" Mr. Crane cheered. "OK,

try singing along and clapping to the beat at the same time."

That wasn't so easy. It was hard to stay together. Winston kept clapping too fast, and Caroline Pearce forgot the words.

Mr. Crane smiled. "That was pretty good. Now we'll add the instruments." He carried the box around for kids to choose.

Lila and Eva chose maracas. Julie and Todd took the triangles. Lois Waller, Caroline, Ellen, Tom McKay, and Andy Franklin grabbed fluto-phones. Sandy took the tambourine. Winston took the cymbals. Ricky Capaldo and Kisho took sand blocks. Jim Sturbridge and Amy took wood blocks. Elizabeth took a cowbell. Ken and Charlie took wood sticks. Then Jerry asked for the drum!

I sighed and took the finger cymbals. They were really hard to put on.

Once everyone had an instrument, Mr. Crane quieted us down and played the tape again. "One, two. One, two," he counted. He jumped when Winston banged the cymbals.

When Mr. Crane stopped the music, everyone switched. This time Ken played the drum and I played the cowbell. We kept playing music and switching.

Finally Elizabeth got the drum, and then she passed it to me. It was big, but I liked the soft, hollow sound it made when I hit it with a special drumstick called a mallet.

"Marvelous," Mr. Crane said. "And now for the rest of my surprise!"

"What?" everyone asked at once.

"We're going to play the instruments

and march in the St. Patrick's Day parade!"

"Yay!" everyone shouted.

I was so excited my heart started beating like the drum. *Ka-boom! Ka-boom! Ka-boom!* I raised my hand to ask if I could keep the drum, but Mr. Crane didn't give me a chance.

"Tomorrow we're going to have a little tryout," Mr. Crane said. "That way we can find out which instrument you each play the best."

A tryout? Ugh! Was Mr. Crane actually going to choose someone other than *me* to play the drum?

# CHAPTER 2
# Little Drummer Girl

*Clack! Clack! Clack!*

Winston banged together two spoons he'd found in his cubby. "I saw people playing spoons on TV once," he explained. "Maybe I can play these in the parade."

"And *we'll* play the blocks," Charlie said. He and Jerry added to the noise by banging the wood and sand blocks together as hard as they could. *Bang! Bang! Bang! Scrape! Scrape! Scrape!*

"Yikes!" Elizabeth said.

"Too loud!" Caroline yelled.

"Guys, calm down." Mr. Crane motioned for them to stop playing. "We want to play *music*. Louder doesn't always mean better."

Winston laid down his spoons. "I thought it was good," he said with a pout.

Mr. Crane grinned. "Let's talk about the difference between noise and music."

I knew the difference. Music is pretty. Noise means *boys*.

"I know about music," Lila said. "I've been taking piano lessons. I can read notes and everything." Lila *always* has to be a show-off.

Mr. Crane nodded. "Each instrument has a different sound," he began. "You can really change the mood of a song by playing different instruments or using different tempos."

"What's a tempo?" Winston asked.

"It's the speed of a song," Mr. Crane explained. "The rhythm, the beat—like when we were counting before, remember?"

"One, two. One, two," Winston chanted.

Mr. Crane picked up a flutophone. "Here. I'll show you." He positioned his fingers and blew gently into the instrument. The sound was soft, like a whisper. First he played a slow rhythm: one . . . two . . . one . . . two . . .

And then he sped up: one-two-one-two-one-two!

"If the song is gentle, which tempo would you use?" Mr. Crane asked.

"The slow one," Eva said.

"Right. And if you wanted action or

excitement, which would you use?"

"Fast," Elizabeth answered.

"Right again. What about if you were feeling sad?"

"I'd play a slow song," I said.

"Good. How about if you were happy?"

"Fast," Lila replied.

"Right. But remember, faster doesn't mean louder." He demonstrated by gently and quickly clacking the wood blocks together. "Now let's practice playing the instruments *softly*."

"Won't we have to play loud in the parade so everyone can hear us?" Winston asked.

Mr. Crane nodded again. "For now, let's learn about rhythm. We can turn up the volume later."

The boys looked like they didn't understand.

I giggled. If there's anything boys *aren't,* it's *quiet.*

"I'm going to be the best musician in the class," Lila whispered. "Besides piano, I've been taking dance too, so Mr. Crane will probably ask *me* to help him teach." She grinned and tossed her long brown hair over her shoulder.

I scrunched my face into a frown. Lila is one of my best friends and all, but when she acts like a snob, she makes me mad enough to hiss like a snake.

"*I'm* going to be the star of the parade," I said, jutting my chin in the air. "I'm going to play the drum."

"How do *you* know?" Lila asked, looking smug.

"I just know," I replied.

"*I'm* going to play the drum," Winston said.

Todd shook his head. "No, *I'm* going to. You're too loud, Winston."

I gritted my teeth. There was a whole *box* full of instruments. Why did everyone else want to play the same one as me? If someone else got to play the drum, Lila would make fun of me for the rest of my life.

Elizabeth tapped me on the shoulder. "Jess, the drum was so much fun. I hope I get to play it in the parade!"

I groaned. Now even my twin sister was against me! What was I going to do?

# CHAPTER 3
# Jessica Misses the Beat

One, two. One, two. One, two . . . I repeated the rhythm over and over in my head all night, even while I was supposed to be sleeping. I couldn't mess up in the tryout. I had to play the drum right!

When morning came, my eyes were red and puffy, and I was so tired that I started saying the numbers backward in my head: *Two, one. Two, one. Two, one.*

"Jessica, come on!" Elizabeth yelled. "We're going to be late for school."

I raced outside to the bus. Elizabeth talked to her friends, but I sat by myself and pretended the bus seat was the drum. I kept patting it and trying to keep the rhythm. But every time the bus bounced, I goofed. I was so nervous, my stomach felt like there was Jell-O jiggling around inside.

"I can't wait until the parade," Amy said as we climbed off the bus. "I hope we get to wear something cool, like uniforms."

"I hope they'll be green for St. Patrick's Day." Elizabeth laughed. "It'll be the best parade ever!"

*Not if we have to wear green,* I thought. Green reminded me of spinach. I wanted to wear my new pink dress instead. If I had to wear green *and* play something other than the drum, it would be the *worst* parade ever!

When we shuffled into room 203, everyone was talking about the parade.

"I heard they're going to take pictures of it for the newspaper," Ellen said.

"And there'll be all kinds of floats," Todd said. "One of the classes is dressing like leprechauns, and another one is making shamrock cookies to sell."

Lila grabbed my arm. "Look, I brought in some music so I could show Mr. Crane I can read it," she said.

I looked at the lines and squiggly symbols. It looked like space alien words to me.

Mr. Crane came in and clapped his hands. "Good morning!"

Everyone rushed to their seats.

"Are we going to play the instruments first?" Amy asked.

Mr. Crane shook his head. "Let's finish our math this morning before our tryout."

I pulled out my math book. "How are we supposed to add and subtract when we're thinking about the try-out?" I asked. My worksheet would probably look as squiggly as Lila's music.

"There's nothing to worry about," Mr. Crane replied. "We're just going to play all the instruments and find out which one is best for you. It'll be fun. It's not a test."

Everyone else looked happy, but I groaned. I couldn't help being nervous. I wanted to play that drum more than anything!

As we got to work on our math, the rhythm I'd been practicing popped in my head. It was hard not to write

"One, two. One, two." for all the answers.

Finally, a half hour later, Mr. Crane collected our worksheets. "Now it's music time," he announced.

Everyone cheered. I chewed my fingernail.

"I hope I get to play the maracas," Eva said.

Ellen tossed her hair. "I want to play the flutophone."

"I want the sand blocks," Todd announced.

"I want the wood sticks." Winston clicked two pencils together.

"I thought you wanted to play the drum," Elizabeth said.

"I changed my mind," Winston replied. "I practiced the sticks out in my yard last night. I was so good I put my cat, Friskie, to sleep."

"She probably ran away and hid," I whispered to Ellen. Ellen giggled.

"OK, we have several pairs of sticks but only one pair of cymbals. Does anyone want to try the cymbals?" Mr. Crane asked.

Winston raised his hand.

"You just said you wanted to play the sticks!" Amy cried.

"I want to keep all my bases covered," Winston replied.

Lila shook her head. "You're the biggest goofball in the world, Winston."

Mr. Crane handed Winston the cymbals and started the music. Only this time it wasn't "The Muffin Man." It was an Irish song called "When Irish Eyes Are Smiling." I'd never heard it before.

Winston smiled as he played the cymbals. *Crash! Crash!* He even marched around the room in a circle. He made trying out look like a lot of fun.

"Good work, Winston," Mr. Crane said. "It looks like the cymbals are for you. Now, if anyone would like to play blocks or sticks, come up and take a set."

Charlie, Jerry, and Kisho took the blocks. Ken, Ricky, and Sandy chose sticks.

Mr. Crane patted his leg with the beat, and the kids hit the sticks and blocks together. Charlie and Jerry played too fast at first, but finally they caught on.

"Great job," Mr. Crane said. "Now, how about the flutophones?"

Lila picked one up. It was slender and black and pretty. Lois joined her.

Mr. Crane started the music. Lois blew through the instrument, but she blew so hard, it sounded horrible.

"It's harder than I thought," Lois said. Her face turned red.

"Maybe you could try the tambourine," Mr. Crane suggested.

Lois picked up a tambourine and tapped along with the song while Lila played the flutophone. Lois didn't hit the tambourine too hard or too soft, and Lila's playing was perfect.

"Good work, you two," Mr. Crane said when the song was over. "That was excellent."

Lila grinned and strutted back to her seat. But before she sat down, she turned to me and curtsied. What a show-off!

"See, I told you I would be the best," Lila said.

"I don't care," I whispered. "The flutophone is *boooring*."

"It is not!"

"Girls." Mr. Crane shot us a warning look. "Now let's try the drum."

Elizabeth waved her hand in the air. So did I.

"OK, Elizabeth, you go first," Mr. Crane said. "Then we'll let your sister have a turn."

Elizabeth walked up front, and Mr. Crane helped her strap on the drum.

My stomach felt jittery again. I was so nervous, I thought I was going to be sick. Half of me didn't want Elizabeth to mess up. But the other half hoped she would!

Mr. Crane started the tape. Elizabeth tapped the drum softly, keeping perfect time with the music. When the song was over, everyone clapped.

"OK, Jessica," Mr. Crane said. "Your turn."

My legs felt like rubber bands as I walked up front. When Elizabeth handed me the drum, my hands shook. I hoped Mr. Crane couldn't tell how nervous I was as he helped me put on the straps.

"OK, here goes." Mr. Crane turned on the music, but I forgot to move. I was so afraid I'd play it wrong, I froze.

Charlie giggled, and Jerry joined in. They could be so mean sometimes!

"Guys, we'll have none of that, OK?" Mr. Crane told them. Then he gave me a kind smile. "Let's give it another try." He replayed the tape.

I swallowed and tapped the drum. *One, two. One, two.*

*Boom, boom. Boom, boom!* I hit the drum so hard I felt it shake. I hoped I hadn't broken it.

Mr. Crane stopped the tape. "This beat is a little different, Jessica. Listen to the music and play along with it."

I took a deep breath and tried again. *Thump-thump-thump-thump-thump . . .* too fast!

Suddenly I got so nervous that my hand slipped and hit the strap to the drum. The strap snapped and hit the drum, making a *boooiiinggg* sound like I'd heard in a cartoon once. Heat climbed up my neck, and my face was on fire with embarrassment.

Mr. Crane patted me on the shoulder. "That's OK, Jessica. There are plenty of other instruments you can try."

Tears stung my eyes, but I blinked them back. I couldn't believe I'd messed up like that in front of everybody!

"Why don't you try the flutophone?" Lila suggested.

Mr. Crane nodded in agreement. "You did a great job with the flutophone the other day, Jessica. Here— take one and practice. You can try out later."

My feet felt so heavy, I could hardly walk back to my desk. They felt like they had bowling balls sitting on top of them.

My own twin was going to play *my* drum.

And I was stuck with the boring flutophone!

# CHAPTER 4

# Another Drum Idea

"OK, class," Mr. Crane said. "Everyone grab your instruments and line up in the hall, just like we practiced. Let's go through the song together."

The instruments clinked and clanked as we headed into the hall. Mr. Crane started the tape. Music floated through the air.

I pressed my fingers over the holes of the flutophone and blew into the mouthpiece, but I didn't have any energy. Since I wasn't blowing very hard, my flutophone barely made a sound. Its soft, whispery music was drowned out by the other flutophones, the tambourine, the wood blocks and sticks . . . and most of all, the drum!

I kept watching Elizabeth, wishing I were her. When she led us marching up and down the hall, my feet felt as if they'd been cemented to the floor.

"Wonderful," Mr. Crane said when the song was over.

Elizabeth grinned, Lila curtsied, and Ellen twirled her flutophone like a baton. When Winston banged the cymbals and Julie hit the cowbell, Mr. Crane reminded us it was almost time to go home. He told each of us how to carry our instruments home if we wanted to practice. Mr. Crane wouldn't let Elizabeth take the drum home; he said it was too big. She'd need our mom or dad to help bring it home.

Lucky for her. If she'd brought it home, I would have stolen it!

That night at the dinner table, Elizabeth said, "Guess what?"

"You and Jessica are flying to Mars and you're not coming back?" our older brother, Steven, asked hopefully.

Elizabeth shook her head. "No, silly. You remember how Jessica and I are going to be in the St. Patrick's Day parade?"

"Yes," Mom replied as she served us some spaghetti.

"I know. You're going to turn into leprechauns and disappear!" Steven said.

"*No!*" Elizabeth and I yelled.

"Your class is going to be marching and playing instruments, right?" Dad asked.

Elizabeth nodded. "I'm going to play the drum and lead the parade!" She was so excited, her voice sounded squeaky.

"That's great, Liz!" Mom said.

Dad patted her back. "Good for you."

"I heard Jessica bombed when she played the drum," Steven said teasingly. "How hard can it be? All you have to do is pound on it. *Anyone* can do that."

"Steven, don't tease your sister,"

34

Mom warned. "You should apologize for saying that."

"I'm sorry," Steven said. Then he kicked me under the table.

I stuck out my tongue at him.

"Jess is playing the flutophone," Elizabeth said. "She's really good at it."

"She just doesn't have enough rhythm to play the drum," Steven teased.

"Steven, please," Dad said. "Eat your dinner."

Steven stuffed his mouth with bread.

I twirled spaghetti around on my fork and realized how much the noodles looked like worms. They'd look really funny sticking out of Steven's hair.

While Elizabeth

talked about the drum, I thought about what Steven had said. I *had* bombed, but that was only because I was so nervous. I was sure that if I had another chance, I could play the drum better.

When dinner was over, I grabbed Elizabeth's hand and pulled her outside underneath the big pine tree. We like to go there to tell secrets.

"What is it?" Elizabeth asked as she sat down.

"I have an idea." I smiled just thinking about it. "You know how much I want to play the drum in the parade."

Elizabeth nodded. "But Mr. Crane wants you to play the flutophone."

"That's only because I goofed during the tryout."

"So?" Elizabeth looked at me suspiciously.

"*So,* I *know* I could play the drum better than the flutophone."

Elizabeth frowned. "How do you know that?"

"Because I was nervous. My hands were shaking and I felt all wiggly."

"But I'm playing the drum now," Elizabeth argued. "Mr. Crane said so."

"I know. So we can switch!" I clapped my hands in excitement. "I'll be you and you'll be me. It'll be fun. We can trade instruments and no one will ever know."

"But we'll get in trouble if Mr. Crane finds out."

"No one will find out. I promise." I tugged at her hands. "Oh, please, Lizzie. I *really* want to play the drum."

"So do I," Elizabeth complained.

"Oh, please, *please,* Lizzie. Lila was bragging and said she was going to be the star of the show. Then I told her *I* was because I'd be playing the drum. And now I'm not—"

"OK, OK," Elizabeth said with a laugh. "You win. We'll switch."

"Really?"

"Really." She smiled. "It's more important to you than it is to me. I'd be happy to play the flutophone."

"Secret promise sign?"

Elizabeth laughed. "Secret promise sign." She crossed her heart and snapped her fingers twice. I did the same.

For a minute I was afraid that I'd hurt Elizabeth's feelings. But when I hugged Elizabeth, she smiled. She wasn't mad at me at all!

"You're the best twin sister ever, Lizzie!"

"OK, but you owe me big time."

We giggled and ran back to the house hand in hand.

That night, when I finally went to sleep, I dreamed about being a great musician. Spotlights shone on me. Everyone wanted my picture and my autograph.

When I woke up, I hopped out of bed. Elizabeth didn't even have to yell at me for being late. In fact, I made it to the bus before she did. I actually couldn't wait to get to school!

# CHAPTER 5
# The Twin Switch

"Psst, Lizzie," I whispered. I didn't want anyone on the bus to know that my twin and I had switched places. I was even wearing a blue shirt that day. Blue is Elizabeth's favorite color. And Elizabeth was wearing pink, my favorite. But I had just noticed something that could give us away!

Elizabeth leaned over. "Don't call me that, *Elizabeth*."

"I know, Li—uh, Jess," I hissed. "But look at our name bracelets. We forgot to switch them!"

Elizabeth's eyes grew wide. "We'd better take them off."

"Good idea." We both slipped off our name bracelets and stuck them in our book bags.

About fifteen minutes later, we were walking into room 203. Mr. Crane had art supplies sitting on the tables.

"Aren't we going to practice?" I asked. I *had* to practice. I couldn't wait to get my hands on the drum again!

"Yes," Mr. Crane said. "But first we're going to make St. Patrick's Day decorations."

"Fun!" Ellen said.

"Can we make shamrocks?" Eva asked.

"Sure." Mr. Crane pointed to the supplies. "There's construction paper for shamrocks and paint for a big mural. I thought we'd work together to paint a rainbow."

"Cool," Todd said.

"I have materials for everyone to make hats too." Mr. Crane showed us how to make a top hat out of paper. "We'll put yarn through each end to tie it on."

For the next hour, Elizabeth and I worked on cutting out shamrocks and gluing streamers and decorations on the paper hats. We were super careful not to call each other by our real names.

When we were finished, everyone modeled their silly hats. Winston had stuck feathers on his. He looked like he had a green chicken on his head.

Charlie and Jerry had hung shamrocks on each side of theirs. They looked like they had big, green leprechaun ears.

Then we took turns painting a rainbow on a huge piece of paper. I painted the red part of the rainbow and stood back to admire it. I could just picture all of us marching past the mural right in the middle of town. I'd be playing the drum, and a photographer would snap my picture in front of the pretty colors. That night I'd see myself on TV leading the entire parade. The headline in the paper would read "Little Drummer Girl" in big bold letters. I could hardly wait!

Art time was over, so after we all cleaned up it was *finally* time for rehearsal. "Everyone, get your instruments and take your place in the hall, please," Mr. Crane announced.

We hurried to our spots. Elizabeth held the flutophone to her mouth and smiled at me. I winked at her and picked up the mallet with shaking fingers, ready to begin.

"One, two. One, two," Mr. Crane murmured.

Everyone straightened and held their instruments, ready to play. Then Mr. Crane pushed the play button on the tape player. My hands were shaking so badly, I almost hit the drum before the tape started!

Finally the music began. *Wham!* I hit

the drum too hard! It made a loud *booooom* sound that echoed through the hall like thunder.

Mr. Crane wrinkled his nose, but he didn't say anything. He just asked us to try marching and playing at the same time.

I tapped softly and marched. Right, left. Right, left. *Tap, tap, tap, tap-tap, tap-tap-tap, taptaptaptap—*

What was happening? I was tapping faster and faster, and my feet were itching to do a jig. But behind me, the other kids started marching faster and faster too.

Winston ran into Charlie. The cymbals crashed and clattered onto the floor. Charlie ran into Jerry, Jerry bumped Lois, Lois squealed, and Elizabeth and Ellen collided. It was a mess—and it was all my fault!

# CHAPTER 6

# Rehearsal Reversal

"Halt," Mr. Crane said. "Elizabeth, you're speeding up. Try to keep time with the music, OK?"

I looked at Elizabeth for five seconds before I realized Mr. Crane was talking to *me!* I was so upset, I had totally forgotten about the twin switch.

"I'm sorry, Mr. Crane," I apologized, just like my twin would. "I'll play it right this time."

Right, left. Right, left.

*Boom, boom. Boom-boom, boom-boom-boom—*

The drum seemed to get heavier with each step. So I banged louder and marched quicker, really getting into the rhythm of the song. I even started singing along.

"When Irish eyes are smiling . . ."

I sped up, getting more and more excited. Then I looked over my shoulder and saw that everyone else was marching faster too.

They were going to run over me!

I hurried forward and banged harder and faster, harder and faster, until *everyone* was running!

Mr. Crane stopped us again. My cheeks burned with embarrassment. But I wouldn't give up. No way! The drum was mine, and I was going to play it no matter what.

Elizabeth leaned over and whispered in my ear, "Do you want to switch back?"

"Nuh-uh," I said stubbornly. "I'm getting the hang of it. I was *born* to play the drum."

When the music began again, I took a deep breath and watched Mr. Crane as he clapped along. Right, left. Right, left. Right, left, left, right-left—

My feet got confused, and I ran into the wall!

Lois ran into me and dropped her tambourine. It jingled as it rolled across the floor.

Mr. Crane rubbed his hand through his hair. "Elizabeth, I'm not sure the drum is working out for you. Maybe you should try another instrument."

Tears stung the backs of my eyelids. This couldn't be happening *again!*

I gave Elizabeth a nervous look. If she told Mr. Crane about our twin switch, I'd be in *big* trouble. She'd say it was all my idea and—

"Mr. Crane?" Elizabeth raised her hand.

"Yes, Jessica?"

"Elizabeth can handle it," Elizabeth said, grinning at me. "She's just a little nervous today, that's all. I know she can do it."

I smiled at her gratefully. Elizabeth really was the best twin sister in the world!

"OK, Elizabeth," Mr. Crane said to me. "I'll give you another chance. But remember, we have only two days until the parade."

I gulped. Even though Elizabeth had kept our secret, I still had three problems.

#1: I had to learn how to keep the beat and march.

#2: I had to keep the twin switch a secret.

#3: I had just two days till parade time: too short for #1, and too long for #2.

What a mess!

# CHAPTER 7
# Disaster Strikes

"Elizabeth, I think you should practice the drum at home," Mr. Crane suggested the next day after another messy rehearsal.

"I will," I said, trading looks with the real Elizabeth.

"And Jessica," Mr. Crane said to Elizabeth, "you're doing a great job with the flutophone. Would you do a solo for us?"

"A solo?" Elizabeth squeaked. "In the parade?"

"Yes, Jessica. It'll be simple. Just

play a few notes by yourself at this point. . . ." He picked up a flutophone and demonstrated for us. "You'll be the only one playing. Everyone else will stop. Would you like to do it?"

"Sure." Elizabeth grinned and hugged the flutophone.

"Why can't I get a solo too?" Lila whined quietly. "That's not fair, Jessica."

I couldn't believe it—I had a solo in the parade. And I wasn't even the one who would be playing it! No matter what, my twin was going to be the star of the show.

"Now let's go back into the classroom, because there's a special treat waiting there," Mr. Crane said. "The school has some real marching band uniforms for you to wear in the parade."

We all cheered as we ran back into room 203.

"Be sure to try them on when you get home and make sure they fit," Mr. Crane said. "Then hang them up so they don't get wrinkled. Now, when I call your name, come up and get yours."

Todd held up his uniform. "Hey, these are pretty cool."

The pants were white, and the jackets were blue. I wanted to ask if they had any pink jackets, but I bit my tongue. That was something Jessica would have said. And I was supposed to be Elizabeth!

Each uniform came with a goofy-looking hat. The hats were big and white and fuzzy and had chin straps.

Winston plunked his hat on top of his head. It was one of the silliest things

I had ever seen! His hair stuck out everywhere underneath it, and it totally clashed with his orange T-shirt and jeans. He looked like a human Q-Tip.

When the bell rang, Mr. Crane helped me carry the bass drum outside. Mom was waiting for us in the minivan. She hung up our uniforms and carefully put the drum in the back.

"Now remember, Elizabeth, practice that drum tonight," Mr. Crane said, looking straight at me.

Mom frowned in confusion. *Oh, no!* Was Mom going to blow our twin switch?

Luckily, Mr. Crane hurried back into the school before Mom could say a word.

"Girls—"

"Look! We have our uniforms," I blurted out.

"And I'm playing a solo," Elizabeth piped up.

Mom looked confused again. "But I thought *you* were playing the fluto-phone." She pointed to me. "And *you* were playing the drum." She pointed to Elizabeth.

"Oh, we traded," I said, crossing my fingers. I was treading on thin ice. I hate to lie to Mom, so not telling her the whole story seemed like the best thing to do.

At home, Elizabeth and I took our instruments in the den to practice. Elizabeth played the solo perfectly the first time.

I tried to play the drum with her, but I kept forgetting the tune, and I couldn't match the beat.

"What are you doing? Playing a war chant?" Steven said. When I looked up, he had socks on his ears. "It sounds like there's a bunch of elephants stampeding in here."

"I have to practice!" I shouted.

Steven made a face and pressed the socks tighter over his ears. When he walked away, he looked like he had dog ears flopping up and down on the sides of his head.

After dinner, I practiced again. Dad was reading the paper in the den and Mom was studying one of her decorating books, so I decided they would be my audience. I  marched around the room, pounding on the drum.

58

*Boom, boom. Tap-tap-tap. Boom! Tap! Bang! Boooooom!*

When I turned around, my father was bent over, tiptoeing from the room. He was sneaking away from me!

"I have some errands to do," Mom said. She jumped up and ran from the room too. What was wrong? Didn't they like my drum playing?

*Boom, tap. Boom-boom, tap. Bang! Bang!*

I practiced and practiced. The next day at school I was a little better, but not much. I only ran into the wall once, but I tripped over my feet about a dozen times. I was doomed!

Finally it was the night before the parade. I was so nervous that I thought about giving up. I couldn't carry a beat if it had handles! Still, I didn't want to be a quitter. I *had* to be the star of the St. Patrick's Day parade no matter what!

That night I marched up the steps to the bedroom I share with my sister. I practiced as I climbed. I wanted to find Elizabeth so that we could practice some more before the parade.

*Boom, bang*—no. *Tap, tap*—no. *Boooooom! Bang-bang-bang!*

When I walked into our bedroom, Elizabeth didn't even glance up. I marched around the room, banging and pounding some more, but she still didn't notice me. Finally I tapped her on the shoulder.

"How am I doing?"

"*What?*" Elizabeth yelled.

"I said, *how am I doing?*" Why couldn't she hear me?

Elizabeth pulled earplugs out of her ears! Was she wearing them because of me?

My sister flopped back on her bed and groaned. "Ohhh, I don't feel so good." She pressed her hand over her forehead and closed her eyes. "I think I'm getting sick."

I gasped and set the drum on the bed. "You *can't* get sick, Lizzie. Tomorrow's the parade."

Elizabeth groaned again. "But I don't feel good."

"Maybe Mom can give you some medicine," I said frantically.

Elizabeth rolled over and hugged her stuffed koala bear. "I just want to sleep," she said.

Panic bubbled inside me. If Elizabeth was too sick to march in the parade, there wouldn't be anyone to play the flutophone solo. What a disaster! Mr. Crane would be so disappointed.

Then I had an idea. Maybe . . .

maybe *I* could play the flutophone in Elizabeth's place!

I peeked at her again. She moaned, but her eyes were closed. She was already asleep!

I picked up the instrument and played a few notes. The song was a pretty easy one to play—at least it was for me. Elizabeth and I had practiced it together dozens of times. If I could play the flutophone well enough to take Elizabeth's place, maybe Mr. Crane could play the drum. We'd still make a great marching band. In fact, we'd be even better—because I wouldn't be messing everyone up anymore!

While I played the flutophone, I decided to tell Mr. Crane my plan as soon as I got to the parade in the morning. He *had* to help—if he didn't get too angry about the twin switch!

# CHAPTER 8

# Jessica's Jitters

"Ow!" My band uniform was so itchy I kept scratching myself. Plus I was so jittery, I kept jumping and squirming around in the minivan on the way to the parade.

"Settle down," Dad said. "You're going to be fine. I've never seen you so nervous."

My stomach rolled as we parked near the parade start line. I knew that if Dad found out the truth, he wouldn't be so cheerful.

"Come on," Dad urged. "I'll carry

the drum. You bring the flutophone."

When I found my class, everyone was laughing. Some of the kids were scratching themselves too. It made me feel itchy again.

"These suits feel like they've got bugs in them," Winston said. He scratched his head first, then his arms. Then he jumped up and down like a monkey.

*Bugs?* I scratched even harder.

"Look at Mr. Crane!" Charlie yelled.

"Where is he?" Winston craned his neck above the crowd and almost lost his hat. "All I see is the Jolly Green Giant."

Everyone laughed again.

"What is that?" I asked Ellen.

"It's Mr. Crane," she whispered.

64

"He's dressed like a leprechaun."

I stood on my tiptoes and saw him, then burst out laughing. He was wearing green tights and a green leprechaun suit with elflike shoes.

But then I remembered I had to tell him about Elizabeth and the truth about the twin switch. I stopped laughing and suddenly felt sick. But I couldn't let Mr. Crane down—or Elizabeth either. "I have to talk to Mr. Crane," I told my dad.

"OK," Dad said. He kissed me on the forehead and waved good-bye. "Have a good time. We'll be cheering for you."

I began tiptoeing toward Mr. Crane. What was I going to say?

If I kept pretending to be Elizabeth, I could tell him that *Jessica* was sick and that I was going to play the flutophone in her place.

But if I was myself and admitted that Elizabeth was sick, then I could play the flutophone just like he thought I was doing all along.

Either way, I wouldn't have to play the drum. But both ways seemed wrong somehow. I was so confused!

"Hey, Jessica," Mr. Crane said with a smile. "Are you ready for your solo?"

I nodded. He must have thought— uh, *known*—that I was me, because I was holding the flutophone.

My head started spinning. This was getting too crazy! I couldn't figure out who I was supposed to be anymore!

*Should I tell him the truth?* I wondered. If I did, he might punish me by having me sit out the parade. But I couldn't hold it in much longer. I took a deep breath and gathered my courage.

"Mr. Crane, I need to tell you something."

Mr. Crane leaned over. "Yes?"

I squared my shoulders and spilled out the whole story. Mr. Crane had a serious expression on his face when I finished.

"I'm really sorry," I apologized. "I know I shouldn't have tricked you, but I *really* wanted to play the drum." I squirmed. "But I was . . . I was being *selfish*. I should have thought about the whole class and not just myself. I wasn't being fair, and I'm sorry."

Mr. Crane patted my shoulder. "I'm really glad you told me the truth, Jessica. And I accept your apology."

I let out a big breath. "I don't want to let everyone down, Mr. Crane. If I play the flutophone, will you play the drum in my place?"

Mr. Crane narrowed his eyes. "I can't do that, Jessica. After all, you decided to make the switch. You'll just have to grin and bear it!"

My heart sank. I was going to have to play the drum—and wreck the parade! I was going to be the biggest laughingstock in Sweet Valley.

I couldn't play the drum as well as the flutophone, and I knew it. What if I beat the drum too fast again? All the kids in class would start running and bumping into each other. It would be a disaster!

And there wouldn't be a flutophone solo anymore either. Even worse—maybe Mr. Crane would ask *Lila* to play it! I bet she'd still brag about that when we're ninety years old.

"Everyone line up," Mr. Crane said, clapping. All the kids hurried to find their places.

My stomach leaped up into my throat. I wanted to quit. I *had* to quit. Just when I was about to say the magic words, I looked up and saw Elizabeth running toward me with Mom right behind her.

She didn't look sick anymore.

And she was wearing her uniform!

# CHAPTER 9

# The Perfect Parade

"Elizabeth!" I ran over and hugged her. "I can't believe you're here!"

Elizabeth grinned. "I didn't want to miss the parade."

I placed my hand on her forehead. "Are you feeling better?"

"I'm OK. What did you tell Mr. Crane?" she whispered.

"I told him the truth. I asked him to play the drum, but he said I had to play it anyway. Oh, Elizabeth, I'm sorry. I've ruined everything!"

"Listen, Jess," Elizabeth said. "I really wasn't sick at all last night. I just pretended to be sick because you were being so stubborn. I was hoping you'd see what a good flutophone player you are."

"You *tricked* me?" I started to get mad, but then I realized Elizabeth was right. I was a terrible drum player, but the flutophone seemed natural to me. And I really did like the pretty sound of the instrument better than the headachy *thump-thump-thump* of the drum.

Elizabeth pulled at my arm. "Don't be mad, Jess. We're a team. The band won't sound right without both of us."

I smiled. "You're right. We can't let our class down."

Elizabeth bit her lip and stared at her

shoes for a minute, looking nervous. "There's another secret I have to tell you."

"What?"

"I let Mr. Crane in on the switch."

"*Whaaat?*"

Mr. Crane walked up behind me. "I'm glad you figured out which instrument is better for you, Jessica. You know, not everyone can play the flutophone the way you do. You're really special."

I smiled. "Thank you."

Mr. Crane was right. Everybody has their own special talent.

"You learned a valuable lesson about teamwork, didn't you?" Mr. Crane asked.

I nodded. "It takes all the instruments to make the band sound pretty."

"That's right."

Suddenly a whistle blew. Elizabeth and I both jumped in surprise.

"It's time to march!" Mr. Crane shouted. His big green hat bobbed up and down, and he waved a banner with a shamrock on it in the air.

My twin ran to get the drum and lead the parade. I slipped into place with the flutophone. Lila was so happy to see me, she gave me a hug. Then she pointed to her dad, who was holding a video camera.

Mom, Dad, and Steven waved at us from the sidelines.

Elizabeth and I winked at each other. We were a team again!

# CHAPTER 10

# Jessica's Solo Surprise

"When Irish eyes are smiling . . ." *Boom, boom! Tap, tap! Ding-a-ling, ding-a-ling! Toot, toot!*

All the different sounds blended together to make wonderful music. But *I* decided the flutophone was the prettiest!

People dressed in green hats and costumes lined the street and waved to us as we marched. The street was decorated with banners and green balloons. Booths with food and arts and crafts had been set up all along the street.

As we marched and played, cameras

flashed. A man climbed from a truck with the channel five logo painted on the side. We were going to be on TV!

As we neared the end of the song, my hands started to sweat. My legs felt like they were going to fall out from under me.

It was almost time for my solo.

After playing around with the drums so much, would I really be able to play a solo on the flutophone with everyone watching? What if I goofed like I did in class with the drum—right on TV with the whole town watching? Everyone would laugh.

My heart raced. I wanted to hide inside one of the booths. Why did I have to be so stubborn? I needed more practice than just one night.

Elizabeth began beating the drum while Lois shook the tambourine. That was my cue! I thought I was going to faint.

Then Elizabeth turned and smiled, giving me courage. Mr. Crane danced over and tapped me on the head with his leprechaun wand. He whispered, "Good luck."

I took a deep breath. I couldn't let Elizabeth or Mr. Crane or the class down. I had to play. I placed my fingers on the holes, raised the flutophone, and blew. I played the short, peppy little melody loud and clear—and I played it perfectly!

The crowd clapped and cheered. Mom and Dad, who had been marching along on the sidewalk, smiled proudly and waved. Even Steven gave me a thumbs-up.

When I finished, Mr. Crane leaned over and patted my back. "You have a lot to be proud of today, Jessica."

I turned and looked at Elizabeth. Mr. Crane was right. "We both have a lot to be proud of," I whispered. Elizabeth gave me a secret grin and pounded her drum one more time, just for me. And I gave my flutophone an extra toot, just for her!

*Take Our Daughters to Work Day is coming to Sweet Valley! When the twins spend the day with their mom, will they find trouble on the job? Find out in Sweet Valley Kids #76,* **DANGER: TWINS AT WORK!**

# Turn the page for great activities from Elizabeth and Jessica!

# Mr. Crane's Magic
# St. Patrick's Day Pudding

Mr. Crane's magic pudding recipe will help make your St. Patrick's Day party the best ever!

## Here's what you'll need:
1) enough boxes of instant vanilla pudding to serve everyone at your party
2) a large mixing bowl
3) green food coloring
4) serving cups and spoons

## Here's what you do:
1) With help from a grown-up, prepare the vanilla pudding in the large mixing bowl. Be sure to follow the instructions on the box!
2) Chill the large bowl of pudding in the refrigerator. The instructions will tell you how long the pudding should chill.
3) When the pudding is ready to be served, put a few drops of green food coloring in the bottom of each serving cup.

4) Spoon in a helping of pudding into each cup.
5) Serve the cups to your friends and ask them to stir the pudding.
6) Surprise! The pudding will turn green— just like magic!

Serve magic pudding at all your parties! You can use any color of food coloring you wish. Try putting different colors in each cup and watch your friends' faces as each cup of pudding turns a different color of the rainbow.

## You can even use magic pudding as a party game!

1) Choose a special prize color and put it in only one of the cup bottoms.
2) Set the cups out for your friends. No one will know which cup will turn the special prize color.
3) Watch to see whose pudding turns the special prize color. That friend will win a prize!

# Jessica and Elizabeth's Word Search

Jessica and Elizabeth wrote down ten of their favorite words from the story. Then they hid each one either horizontally (side to side) or vertically (up and down) in the word search puzzle at the bottom of the page.

Can you find all ten? Good luck!

| | |
|---|---|
| BEAT | PARADE |
| CYMBAL | RHYTHM |
| LEPRECHAUN | SHAMROCK |
| MARCH | TAMBOURINE |
| MUSICIAN | TEMPO |

```
B  I  Y  R  W  R  H  Y  T  H  M  X
S  P  I  M  H  U  R  L  N  C  Y  T
H  S  U  M  I  P  M  C  D  L  C  A
A  O  M  M  N  W  B  Y  V  E  U  M
M  M  A  R  C  H  N  M  T  P  E  B
R  T  B  U  W  P  O  B  N  R  C  O
O  X  E  I  P  A  R  A  D  E  P  U
C  M  A  W  T  Y  I  L  R  C  T  R
K  U  T  E  M  P  O  I  B  H  C  I
C  Y  N  I  P  T  M  H  U  A  Z  N
M  U  S  I  C  I  A  N  V  U  I  E
T  E  P  M  E  Q  U  B  F  N  M  C
```

# Answers to Jessica and Elizabeth's Word Search

```
B  I  Y  R  W  R  H  Y  T  H  M  X
S  P  I  M  H  U  R  L  N  C  Y  T
H  S  U  M  I  P  M  C  D  L  C  A
A  O  M  M  N  W  B  Y  V  E  U  M
M  A  R  C  H  N  M  T  P  E  B
R  T  B  U  W  P  O  B  N  R  C  O
O  X  E  I  P  A  R  A  D  E  P  U
C  M  A  W  T  Y  I  L  R  C  T  R
K  U  T  E  M  P  O  I  B  H  C  I
C  Y  N  I  P  T  M  H  U  A  Z  N
M  U  S  I  C  I  A  N  V  U  I  E
T  E  P  M  E  Q  U  B  F  N  M  C
```

## SIGN UP FOR THE SWEET VALLEY HIGH® FAN CLUB!

Hey, girls! Get all the gossip on Sweet Valley High's® most popular teenagers when you join our fantastic Fan Club! As a member, you'll get all of this really cool stuff:

- Membership Card with your own personal Fan Club ID number
- A Sweet Valley High® Secret Treasure Box
- Sweet Valley High® Stationery
- Official Fan Club Pencil (for secret note writing!)
- Three Bookmarks
- A "Members Only" Door Hanger
- Two Skeins of J. & P. Coats® Embroidery Floss with flower barrette instruction leaflet
- Two editions of *The Oracle* newsletter
- Plus exclusive Sweet Valley High® product offers, special savings, contests, and much more!

---

Be the first to find out what Jessica & Elizabeth Wakefield are up to by joining the Sweet Valley High® Fan Club for the one-year membership fee of only $6.25 each for U.S. residents, $8.25 for Canadian residents (U.S. currency). Includes shipping & handling.

Send a check or money order (do not send cash) made payable to "Sweet Valley High® Fan Club" along with this form to:

**SWEET VALLEY HIGH® FAN CLUB, BOX 3919-B, SCHAUMBURG, IL 60168-3919**

NAME_____
(Please print clearly)

ADDRESS_____

CITY_____ STATE _____ ZIP_____
(Required)

AGE_____ BIRTHDAY_____ /_____ /_____

Offer good while supplies last. Allow 6-8 weeks after check clearance for delivery. Addresses without ZIP codes cannot be honored. Offer good in USA & Canada only. Void where prohibited by law.
©1993 by Francine Pascal                                          LCI-1383-123